A FROG and DOG book

Frog
Meets
Dog

by Janee Trasler

ACORN™
SCHOLASTIC INC.

For Miles, with love from Andy Janee.

Library of Congress Cataloging-in-Publication Data

Names: Trasler, Janee, author, illustrator. Title: Frog meets dog / Janee Trasler.
Description: First edition. | New York : Acorn/Scholastic Inc. 2020. | Audience: Ages 4-6 | Audience: K to Grade 3 | Summary: Dog meets three frogs and would like to play, but Dog is not good at their games of hopping and leaping—but when Dog chases away a bear the frogs decide to welcome Dog into their playtime.
Identifiers: LCCN 2019025345 | ISBN 9781338540390 (paperback) | ISBN 9781338540406 (library binding)
Subjects: LCSH: Frogs—Juvenile fiction. | Dogs—Juvenile fiction. | Friendship—Juvenile fiction. | Play—Juvenile fiction. | CYAC: Frogs—Fiction. | Dogs—Fiction. | Friendship—Fiction. | Play—Fiction.
Classification: LCC PZ7.T6872 Fr 2020 | DDC [E]–dc23 LC record available at https://lccn.loc.gov/2019025345

10 9 8 7 6 5 4   21 22 23 24

Printed in China   62

First edition, May 2020

Edited by Rachel Matson

Book design by Sunny Lee

Dog

Dog wants to play.

Frogs hop. Can Dog hop too?

Hop

Hop

Hop

FLOP

Frogs leap. Can Dog leap too?

Leap

Leap

Leap

Frogs jump. Can Dog jump too?

Jump

Jump

Jump

Dog will play another day.

Dog wants to help.
How can Dog help?

Jump

Jump

Jump

Frogs want to play.

Frogs hop. Can Dog hop too?

Hop

Hop

Hop

33

POP

DROP

Frogs jump.
Can Dog jump too?

Jump

Jump

Jump

BUMP

Frogs leap. Can Dog leap too?

Leap

Leap

Leap

Heap

Sleep

Bzzzzz...

Frog wants to eat.

43

Dog will play another day.

About the Author

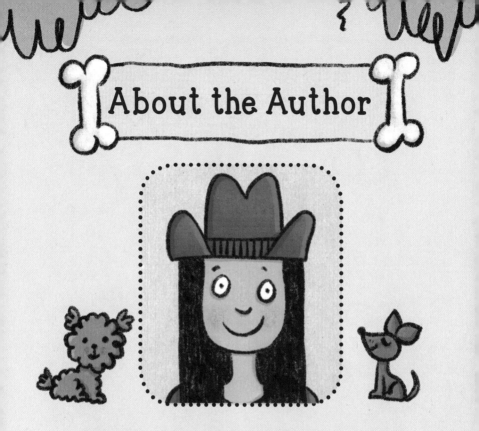

Janee Trasler loves to make kids laugh. Whether she is writing books, drawing pictures, singing songs, or performing with her puppets, she is going for the giggle. Janee lives in Texas with her hubby, her doggies, and one very squeaky guinea pig.

YOU CAN DRAW FROG!

1 Draw a sideways figure 8.

2 Add a dot in the middle of each circle. Draw a "u" for the mouth.

3 Connect the eyes with a big circle for the body.

4 Add an oval on each side for the legs. Draw two little feet.

5 Draw the arms and hands. Be sure to add some speckles!

6 Color in your drawing!

WHAT'S YOUR STORY?

Dog plays with the frogs.
Imagine you are playing with them.
What games would you play together?
Write and draw your story!